ISLA

by ARTHUR DORROS

illustrated by ELISA KLEVEN

PUFFIN BOOKS

PUFFIN BOOKS
Published by the Penguin Group
Penguin Putnam Books for Young Readers, 345 Hudson Street, New York, New York 10014, U.S.A.
Penguin Books Ltd, 27 Wrights Lane, London W8 5TZ, England
Penguin Books Australia Ltd, Ringwood, Victoria, Australia
Penguin Books Canada Ltd, 10 Alcorn Avenue, Toronto, Ontario, Canada M4V 3B2
Penguin Books (N.Z.) Ltd, 182-190 Wairau Road, Auckland 10, New Zealand

Penguin Books Ltd, Registered Offices: Harmondsworth, Middlesex, England

First published in the United States of America by Dutton Children's Books,
a division of Penguin Books USA Inc., 1995
Published by Puffin Books, a member of Penguin Putnam Books for Young Readers, 1999

10 9 8 7 6 5

THE LIBRARY OF CONGRESS HAS CATALOGED THE DUTTON EDITION AS FOLLOWS:
Dorros, Arthur.
Isla/by Arthur Dorros, illustrated by Elisa Kleven.
—1st ed.   p.   cm.
Summary: A young girl and her grandmother take an imaginary journey to the Caribbean island
where her mother grew up and where some of her family still lives.
ISBN 0-525-45149-8
[1. Caribbean Area—Fiction. 2. Islands—Fiction. 3. Grandmothers—Fiction.
4. Hispanic Americans—Fiction.]
I. Kleven, Elisa, ill. II. Title.
PZ7.D7294Is   1995   [E]—dc20 94-40900 CIP AC

Puffin Books ISBN 0-14-056505-1

Manufactured in China

Para los abuelos, Sidney and Debbie,
Harry and Irene Dorros, great storytellers

A.D.

For the Andersen family, and for Saren —
with special thanks to Diana Tejada

E.K.

When Abuela, my grandma,
tells me stories,
we can fly anywhere.
Today she's telling me about *la isla,*
the island where she grew up.
We are flying there together.

We travel a long, long way
to where it is always warm.
"¡Mira!" Abuela calls. *"Mi esmeralda."*
I look. I see her island sparkling like a
green jewel in the sea.
"Aire tropical," says Abuela,
taking a deep breath.
The hot, damp air smells salty.

We fly over forests, fields, and tiny towns
to visit *tío* Fernando, *tía* Isabel, and my cousin Elena.
Even though we're up high,
they see us and wave.

Tío Fernando is my uncle, my *mamá's* brother.

Abuela is their mother.

She raised them on *la isla*.

"¡Bienvenidas!" Tío Fernando welcomes us.
He and my *mamá* grew up in this house
with Abuela and Abuelo, my grandfather.
Abuelo died before I was born.
Now *tío* Fernando lives here with his family.
I think he looks like my *mamá,*
except he has a beard.
"El osito," Abuela calls him — the little bear.

Abuela shows me all around.

In the front room, she and Abuelo

used to run a little store.

On the wall, next to a picture of the store,

is a painting of *tío* Fernando with a giant fish.

"¡Qué pescado!" Abuela says,

telling me what a fish it was.

Tío Fernando found it in a shallow stream.

He brought it home to keep for a pet.

Abuela said the fish would be

happier in the river.

Tío Fernando was sad to see it go,

so Abuela painted the picture for him.

"Los niños," Abuela says,

showing me a picture of some children.

It's my *mamá* and *tío* Fernando

playing in a fountain.

Abuela and Abuelo built the fountain

with stones from the rain forest.

It is still in the yard.

"Es mágica," Abuela says.

The fountain does seem magical.

The water splashing over stones

sounds like birds singing.

Now Abuela wants to show me more of *la isla*.

Elena says she'll meet us later at the beach.

"¡Que disfruten!" she calls. She wants us to have fun.

"Vamos a la selva," says Abuela.
We're going to the rain forest
where the fountain stones came from.
We fly there with parrots
flapping beside us.
The treetops are a bright garden, I tell Abuela.
"Y una sombrilla," Abuela says.
They are an umbrella, too.

Down below, it is dark and cool.
"Como la noche," like night, Abuela tells me.
But she can scoop up a tree frog
or a lizard running on a leaf.

Forest eyes are open wide.

My eyes are open, too.

"Hay mucho más que ver," Abuela says, taking off.

There is much more for us to see.

We fly to the busy old city,
zooming between colored buildings
and over blue brick streets.

Above the square, Abuela and I spin and dip
for the people below.
"Pájaros grandes jugando," Abuela says, and laughs.
We are like big birds playing.

We zoom down to the harbor, where the big ships are.

"De todo el mundo," Abuela tells me.

They come from all over the world.

"*¡Mira!*" She points to a large building.
It was made by Spanish people who
sailed to the island hundreds of years ago.

Abuela and Abuelo used to come to
the city to buy things for their store.
"Ha cambiado," Abuela sighs. The city has changed.
Now there are tall buildings and parking lots
and supermarkets.
"Vamos al viejo mercado," she says.
She wants to go to an old market.
And we do go, soaring above highways…

to an old market in the countryside.
People call out what they are selling:
"*¡Plátanos!*" "*¡Mangos!*" "*¡Papayas!*" "*¡Cocos!*"
"*¡Piñas dulces!*" Abuela calls.

When she was little, her family grew
sweet pineapples to bring to the market.
The market is hot and crowded.
Soon we are ready to cool off.

"*Vamos a nadar,*" Abuela says.
She used to swim here when she was my age.
"*Ven.*" She takes my hand and we dive in.
All kinds of fish flash around us — round fish,
thin fish, fish with stripes, and fish with spots.

Abuela leaps and dives, too.
"Nuestro circo," she says.
We have our own circus.
"Mi pez volador." She tells me
I'm her flying fish.

Tía Isabel, *tío* Fernando, and
cousin Elena join us.
Tío Fernando is wearing his snorkeling goggles.
Abuela jokes that he looks like a forest frog.
We float on our backs, and
the water meets the sky.
We can float anywhere.

When we get home,
we're hungry from our swimming.
"Volemos," Abuela calls.
We fly up into the treetop
to pick ripe mangos.
Our hands get sticky from the syrupy juice.
Abuela picks the ripest ones
for Elena and me.
We'll help make a salad
with mangos and other island fruits.
I'll tell Elena about what I've seen
on her island.

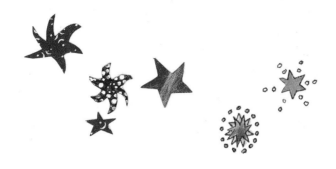

After our meal, we sit out in the garden.
Birds, insects, even frogs are chirping.
"Nos cantan." Abuela says they are singing to us.
The plants around us smell sweet and strong.
It feels like the garden is our room,
with *las estrellas,* the stars, our ceiling.
"Ya es hora de partir," Abuela announces.
It is time to go.
The stars will light our way.

We fly through the night,
back, back, toward home.
When we see New York City,

the lights look like thousands of stars.

"Es mágica," I say to Abuela.

"Sí," she agrees. *"Es mágica."*

After so much flying, we need to sleep.

Abuela asks me what I'm thinking about.

"La isla," I tell her.

"Nuestra isla," she tells me.

I do feel like it is our island.

We can visit it anytime.

"Pronto," Abuela says.

Soon.

GLOSSARY

The capitalized syllable is stressed in pronunciation.

Abuela (ah-BWEH-lah) Grandmother

Abuelo (ah-BWEH-loh) Grandfather

Aire tropical (EYE-reh troh-pee-KAHL)
Tropical air

Bienvenidas (byehn-veh-NEE-dahs) Welcome

Cocos (COH-cohs) Coconuts

Como la noche (COH-moh lah NOH-cheh)
Like the night

De todo el mundo (deh TOH-doh ehl MOON-doh)
From all the world

El osito (ehl oh-SEE-toh) The little bear

Es mágica (ehs MAH-hee-kah) It's magic

Ha cambiado (ah cahm-bee-YAH-doh)
It has changed

Hay mucho más que ver (eye MOO-cho mahs
kay behr)   There is much more to see

La isla (lah EES-lah) The island

Las estrellas (lahs ehs-TREH-yahs) The stars

Los niños (lohs NEE-nyohs) The children

Mamá (mah-MAH) Mama

Mangos (MAHN-gohs) Mangos

Mi esmeralda (mee ehs-meh-RAHL-dah)
My emerald

Mi pez volador (mee pehs voh-lah-DOHR)
My flying fish

Mira (MEE-rah) Look

Nos cantan (nohs CAHN-tahn) They sing to us

Nuestro circo (NWEHS-troh SEER-coh) Our circus

Nuestra isla (NWEHS-trah EES-lah) Our island

Ojos abiertos (OH-hohs ah-BYEHR-tohs)
Eyes open

Pájaros grandes jugando
(PAH-hah-rohs GRAHN-dehs hoo-GAHN-doh)
Big birds playing

Papayas (pah-PIE-yahs) Papayas

Piñas dulces (PEE-nyahs DOOL-sehs)
Sweet pineapples

Plátanos (PLAH-tah-nohs) Plantains

Pronto (PROHN-toh) Soon

Que disfruten (kay dees-FROO-tehn) Enjoy

Qué pescado (kay pehs-KAH-doh) What a fish

Sí (see) Yes

Tía (TEE-ah) Aunt

Tío (TEE-oh) Uncle

Vamos a la selva (BAH-mohs ah lah SELL-vah)
Let's go to the forest

Vamos a nadar (BAH-mohs ah nah-DAHR)
Let's go swimming

Vamos al viejo mercado
(BAH-mohs ahl bee-YEH-hoh mehr-CAH-doh)
Let's go to an old market

Ven (behn) Come

Volemos (boh-LEH-mohs) Let's fly

Y una sombrilla (ee OO-nah sohm-BREE-yah)
And an umbrella

Ya es hora de partir
(yah ehs OH-rah deh pahr-TEER)
Now it is time to leave